I am honored to be able to write about this wonderful story of truth! A much needed book from someone who not only knows God's word but walks it out. Wh t love in a way all ages can understand. This book just makes me smile! It will with children and grandchildren!

Dr. Pamela Legate

The "Kingdom of Kings" is a beautiful children's tale that is told with rare insight, wisdom and artistry. The author Candy Fothergill, in her pioneer effort, displays the talents of a poet, visionary and true lover of children by weaving seamlessly the elements of fantasy, learning and inspiration. The book is beautifully illustrated as well, and joins the narrative to draw the reader along in a peaceful journey of possibility and passion. One could easily imagine children of all ages reading this book again and again. I highly recommend this book and can't wait to see the many beautiful stories that are destined to flow from this talented author with a clear mother's heart!

Phil Wynn
Director of Ascended Life Ministries

"A Kingdom of Kings" is a colorful display of the King and his kingdom value for empowerment. The story here is unique, in that, the one in authority is truly focused on making his subordinates great. The reader is given the opportunity to expand their perspective by a king who prefers his subjects over the authoritative lifestyle we normally see from a royal. This book allows the reader to open their mind to the possibility of sound, light and color, and how the three interact with humanity. The representation of the king's joyfulness with the people is superb and the imagery of the throne is magnificent. Pulling together the understanding of a kingdom of kings with the crowning of the children is a profound climactic moment. The moment builds throughout the story with the interaction amongst the king and his people, to the coronation of the people by the king, wow! The book invites you in, appearing to focus on the king from the perspective of the kingdom, however, the illustration is presented from the king's perspective throughout. I thoroughly enjoyed this piece and have enjoyed observing the awakening of children to the twists and turns of a kingdom of kings. It is transforming to watch children hear and receive that they could be crowned kings in a kingdom of joy and color. Well done!

Beth Cooper, Founder
Uncorked Ministries, LLC

What a refreshing book, " A Kingdom of Kings" is. Candy Forthergill has done a wonderful job of bringing Kingdom understanding to even the youngest of Kingdom subjects. Written and illustrated in such a way so as to give insight but to also cause questions in the little inquiring minds. You will enjoy reading this book with your children as you help them to understand their most important relationship with Father God and their inheritance in the Family of the Father of us all. What incredible love the Father has shown each of us in being called His children. Father's love is so greatly evidenced in Him calling us to rule alongside of Him as "A Kingdom of Kings."

Gaye Rogers
Apostolic Vision Keeper of Healing House
Apostolic Women Arising

A Kingdom of Kings

A Kingdom of Kings

Candy M. Fothergill

Illustrated by
Allison Wynn

XULON PRESS

Xulon Press
2301 Lucien Way #415
Maitland, FL 32751
407.339.4217
www.xulonpress.com

Printed in the United States of America.

Paperback ISBN-13: 978-1-66282-704-4

Once Upon a Time, There was a King who
lived in the most powerful kingdom of all.

His kingdom was the oldest kingdom.
His kingdom was the largest kingdom.
His kingdom was the richest kingdom.
His kingdom was the most beautiful kingdom.

The king was loved by all the people.
He loved them too and could not wait to see them.

He had royal feasts and sent out the decrees.
Everyone came, by ones, twos, and by threes!

The people dressed up in their finest things;
To look their best when they see the king.

N
W
E
S

They came from the north.
They came from the south.
They came from the east.
They came from the west.
They all came as the kings honored guests.

The king loved the people more than the kingdom.
He sent out the royal host to meet them.
As they entered the castle they started to sing;
Through the inner courts to meet with their king.

The people saw the king face to face.
As he sat on the throne that he called grace.
His throne was surrounded by a bright shining rainbow.
With colors so bold they made the whole kingdom glow.

Red, orange, yellow, green, blue, indigo, and violet,
Were the seven colors of the kings' covenant promise.

The king was seated upon his throne;
With a smile that made everyone feel right at home.
There was so much joy as he talked to the people.
Just being with him made everyone feel peaceful.

The king would walk with the people in the beautiful fields.
Saying “the harvest is ready, see it white with its yield”.
He would climb the mountains as he talked with them;
About every part of this growing kingdom.

They would go down to the lake and get in the boat.
The king enjoyed fishing but loved laughing the most!
There are lots of fish to be caught it is true,
But the fish are only as happy as you.

The king would visit their houses and play with the kids.
This was the favorite thing the king did.
The children's laughter was the kings favorite sound.
So he played with them a game where each wore his crown.

When the game was over, he crowned the one winning.
The king thought to himself, "this is only the beginning".
So happy were the children wearing his crown on their head.
"Not only the children, but all the people," he said.

Each person should know how special he thought them to be.
The king said “I’ll make a crown for everyone, indeed”.
Each son and daughter had a crown like no other.
There was a crown for each father, a crown for each mother.
No two crowns in the kingdom were the same.
Each persons was unique as he called them by name.

When the last person of the kingdom was crowned by the king;
He looked around at the people and began to think.

The king looked out at what he had done
He said to himself, “this is very good”.

For he never wanted just a kingdom as a king.

In his heart it was always meant to be

A KINGDOM OF KINGS...!!!

CPSIA information can be obtained
at www.ICGtesting.com
Printed in the USA
LVRC081111220921
698455LV00003B/138